# Martin Chatterton

# STUNT MONKEYS

## STUNT MANIA!

WARNING!

Have you ever tried swimming with a tankful of Amazonian Bone-cutter piranhas?

Or turned your friend into a giant bouncing basketball and shot him through a hoop?

Or come up with a stinky recipe so noxious that it makes everyone barf **INSTANTLY?**

**You haven't?**

**Don't worry!**

**The only people stupid enough to try things as weird as that are...**

# ...THE STUNT MONKEYS!

## STENCH
Can reach speeds of forty kmph through farting alone. Just make sure you're not standing behind him...

## KURTIS
It could be argued that Kurtis is the brains of the group ... which isn't saying much.

## EINSTEIN

Einstein might look like a genius, but this is far from true. He is, however, a master at inventing useless objects.

## GRUNT

The pocket rocket – just point him at the nearest trouble and stand well back. No batteries required.

After the Stunt Monkeys had broken the World Record for Elastic-Propelled Synchronized Flying Elvises (but accidentally demolished the sludge storage towers, covering Sludgeville Arena, Mayor McFoodle, Assistant Pink and the Grand Sludgemaster in three metres of completely stinky sludge), the boys had been forced to lie low.

Sludgeville Council gave them a fine so big that Einstein's calculator ran out of space figuring out how long it would take their parents to pay it off. The answer was never.

And, of course, there were to be absolutely no more attempts to get into The League of Unbelievable and Amazing World Records book.

But it could have been worse. Mayor McFoodle had wanted to throw them to the council bear. Fortunately for the Stunt Monkeys, Assistant Pink told the mayor that feeding children to ferocious animals was against the law.

It was around about that time that the Stunt Monkeys went into hiding and Mayor McFoodle went bananas.

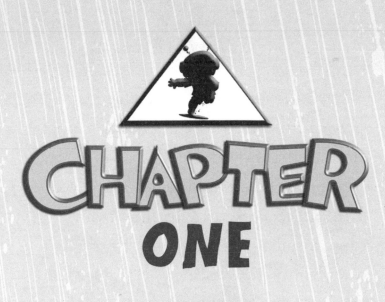

# CHAPTER ONE

## A VISITOR

It was a day like any other in Sludgeville – dull. The Stunt Monkeys sat in their hiding place, in the basement of Sludgeville Town Hall, bored stupid.

It was Kurtis who had come up with the idea of hiding out there. "It's right under their noses!" he'd said.

"They'll never think of looking here!"

And he'd been right. For the past six months they'd hidden in the Town Hall's dingy basement, leaving only at night to pick up supplies from their families. The bathroom was quite amazingly pongy, but they all agreed it was better than the council bear pit.

The only trouble was the boredom. And the smell. Stench let out another silent but deadly fart. It drifted up and joined a number of its friends floating in a dark cloud somewhere near the ceiling.

From over in a corner, Tim, Stench's pet vulture, coughed as he chewed on the remains of a squashed hedgehog Stench had found in the street last night.

Stench reached over to open a small, street-level window so that Tim could breathe. The damp, grey Sludgeville air oozed in.

"I don't know what's worse," said Kurtis. "The stink in here, or the smell out there."

"I can't smell a thing," said Grunt.

"You cannot be serious!" Einstein held his fingers to his nose and checked the Smell-O-Meter he'd made from an old washing-up liquid bottle and a piece of garden hose. He held it up to show the others.

"According to my Smell-O-Meter, it stinks down here! We can't go on like this!" he moaned.

# How to make your very own
# SMELL-O-METER!

Do you live with someone whose bottom is smellier than it should be,
or who only changes their socks when they have to be chipped off?
Then the **SMELL-O-METER** is for you! Just follow these easy to
understand instructions and you'll soon be able to measure
exactly how toxic your environment has become!

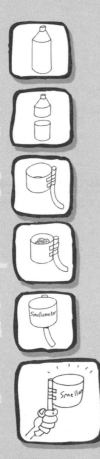

1. Take one empty, dry washing-up liquid bottle.

2. Carefully cut it in half (see diagram).

3. Attach a short length of garden hose (see fig. 3) using sticky tape as shown.

4. Add four figs (see fig. 4). They don't do anything, but it's a funny joke.

5. Write 'Smell-O-Meter' on the side of the bottle.

6. Bingo! You are now the proud owner of another completely useless Einstein invention.

"How long are we going to stay down here?" asked Grunt.

"As long as it takes, I guess," said Kurtis. "No more than a couple of years."

A siren whooped past the window – the Grass Inspection team was on its way to check another poor person's grass.

"Don't they ever give up?" asked Grunt. "I thought after McFoodle went cuckoo Sludgeville would, y'know, run out of rules or something."

"Not a chance," said Kurtis. "I heard he'd left so many spare rules behind that Assistant Pink can run the town for years without him.

Sludgeville's going to be like this for ever! We may as well face it – the Stunt Monkeys are finished. Perhaps we should hand ourselves in."

Stench shrugged his shoulders miserably and began to climb out of the window.

"No, Stench," said Kurtis hauling him back inside. "That's not the answer."

"Then what is?" said Einstein.

"Television!" said a strange voice from the doorway. "Television's the answer to all your troubles, boys!"

Standing in the doorway was a skinny man dressed from head to toe in black and carrying a leather briefcase. He stepped into the basement and smiled a big television smile.

"It took a while, boys," he said. "But we finally found you!"

"That's all very well," said Grunt. "But who are you exactly?"

The man made a bow.

"I'm Jeremy Smashing, a producer at Channel Sludge. And I might just be about to save your lives!"

# CHAPTER
## TWO

### GENTLE LANDINGS

Over on the other side of Sludgeville, it was visiting time at the Gentle Landings Rest Home for The Very Very Nervous.

Assistant Pink sat next to his boss as they watched the Channel Sludge evening news. The once mighty Mayor McFoodle, in pyjamas and a

ratty old bathrobe, rocked back and forth, muttering nasty words under his breath, his eyes never leaving the screen.

"Have a sweetie, Your Worship," said Assistant Pink. "You like sweeties, remember?"

He pushed a boiled sweet into Mayor McFoodle's mouth and sighed.

His boss had been like this ever since those stupid boys had ruined SludgeFest 50. It would have been the biggest day of Horace T. McFoodle's life if …
if it hadn't been for those blasted Stunt Monkeys! Pink shuddered as he remembered the wave of sludge washing over the Grand Sludgemaster and all the other important people. It had been horrible. The Grand Sludgemaster had to be hosed down by the fire brigade, and had vowed never to set foot in Sludgeville ever again.

"Never mind, Your Magnificence,"
he murmured. "Revenge will be
ours, I swear it!"

Pink pushed another sweet into
Mayor McFoodle's mouth and
brushed some crumbs off his
pyjamas. He sat back and settled
down for another long evening
watching people arguing on
television. Nothing seemed to get
through to the Mayor. The doctor
had explained that the shock of The
Great SludgeFest Disaster had
locked him into a sort of trance.

"It's possible that another shock
might just jolt him back to his old
self," Professor Bloke had said.
"But then again he could remain like

this for the rest of his life."

Assistant Pink was thinking about this when Mayor McFoodle gave a sudden strangled screech and jumped up.

"Look! LOOK PINK!" he screamed, pointing at the screen with one hand and clutching Pink's sleeve with the other. "It's them! THEM!"

Pink followed Mayor McFoodle's finger and looked at the TV.

A blond-haired presenter with a goatee beard was grinning into the camera. Behind him were four familiar-looking boys.

"Oh, sir!" said Pink. "You're back! Talking! This is wonderful!"

"Never mind that, you fool! Look! It's those blasted Munt Stunkeys – I mean Stunt Monkeys!" shouted Mayor McFoodle, bouncing up and down like a yo-yo. "I thought you said you couldn't find those idiot boys anywhere!"

"I don't understand, Your Worship! I sent a hand-picked squad of Ninja Traffic Wardens to track them down

and a crack team of Undercover
Litter Monitors as back up! In six
months we've turned up nothing."

"Yet here they are, on my TV!"
cried McFoodle, glued to
the screen.

"Welcome to the KRAY-
ZEE-EST show on Channel
Sludge!" yelped the
presenter. "My name's
Simon Fudge-Smythe, and over the
next few weeks we'll be going
completely STUNT-TASTIC right here
in Sludgeville! Which is where these
boys come in! Some of you may
remember that little mishap at
SludgeFest 50 last year – by the way,
how funny was that?!"

"Funny? Funny? He thinks it was FUNNY?" McFoodle ground his teeth.

On screen, the presenter carried on, his smile flashing brightly.

"Well, the boys responsible for that hilarious disaster have been in hiding ever since. But, guess what? Channel Sludge has tracked them down, paid off all the damage, cleared them with the courts and brought them back to Sludgeville for four weeks of uninterrupted WORLD RECORD STUNT MADNESS! So, without further ado, ladies and gentlemen, boys and girls, allow me to introduce Kurtis! Grunt! Einstein! And, last but not least, Stench! Better known as THE STUNT MONKEYS!"

# STUNT MONKEYS

The boys stepped forward. Grunt stood on his hands and waved a foot, Stench hovered a couple of feet off the floor using fart power, Kurtis juggled six flaming chainsaws while blowing a large bubblegum bubble, and Einstein just waved.

As the cheers died down, Simon stepped back into shot. "Tune in at 6.30pm tomorrow to see some of the most bonkers stunts ever attempted on TV!" he screeched. There was a final blast of music, then an advert for soap filled the screen.

Mayor McFoodle looked like he was about to erupt.

"Get me my clothes, Pink!" he snapped. "And my best chain. We've got some urgent council business to take care of!"

"Yes, sir!" breathed Pink smiling broadly. "Right away, Your Excellency! It's lovely to see you back to your old self!"

# CHAPTER THREE

## STUNT MANIA!

"I thought it was going to be bigger than this," said Grunt, looking around Studio 7 at Channel Sludge during a break in filming. "More, I dunno, posh."

Studio 7 certainly didn't look very posh. It looked small and dirty. Thick, dusty black cables snaked

across the floor and hung down in bunches from the roof. Lights were everywhere; big, hot lights that gave off a sour burnt-metal smell.

Two bored-looking cameramen wearing Stunt Monkey T-shirts stood next to their cameras waiting for instructions and munching stale ham sandwiches.

"Chop chop people!" yelled a skinny man as he strode through the studio. It was Jeremy Smashing, the producer.

"TV waits for no one!" he said, shooing Einstein, Kurtis, Grunt and Stench towards the most brightly-lit area of the set.

It was day one of *Stunt Mania!* and the Stunt Monkeys were about to attempt their first ever televised stunt.

"I feel sick," said Einstein. "I don't think I can do this TV thing. It's making me nervous! I need the loo!"

"Oh shut up, Einstein!" said Grunt. "How hard can it be?"

"I don't know," said Kurtis, eyeing
the props waiting for them. "Looks
pretty hard from where I'm standing.
Why didn't they ask us to come up
with ideas?"

"Well, boys," said Jeremy, joining
them on stage. "What do you think?"

Standing in the middle of Studio 7
were two large tanks of water. One
contained only water. A large shoal
of square-looking fish swam round
and round inside the other.

"Doesn't look that bad to me," said Grunt. "Tank full of goldfish. Don't see what the problem is."

Kurtis hoicked a ham sandwich out of the mouth of a nearby cameraman and, ignoring the cameraman's shout, tossed it into the tank. Immediately, the water boiled as the fish attacked the sandwich in a frantic finny frenzy. Einstein gulped.

"The problem is," said Kurtis, "they ain't goldfish. They're piranhas."

"Amazonian Bone-cutter piranhas to be precise," grinned Jeremy. "Took us ages to track the little devils down!"

Grunt stepped forward and tapped the tank.

"And how, exactly, do we fit in?"

Jeremy looked a bit surprised.

"Oh dear. Hasn't anyone from Production gone through this with you?" He shook his head and tapped a thin finger on his clipboard. "It's right here on the running order: 'Item One – Stunt Monkeys attempt first ever televised **World Record for Underwater Speed Piranha Rodeo**'."

Stench parped noisily.

Bonus Freaky Fact!

In some parts of Brazil, scissors are called 'piranhas'.

"It's quite straightforward," said
Jeremy. "You shin up the ladder, pop
into the tank, chuck the fish into the
empty tank and hop back out again."

"'Hop' being the right word,"
said Einstein. "On account of
us HAVING ONLY ONE LEG
LEFT! If we're lucky!"

"How do we stop ourselves
getting eaten, Jeremy?" said Kurtis.

"I really have no idea," said
Jeremy, a puzzled look on his face.
"I thought that was rather your
department, seeing as you're the
actual Stunt Monkeys. Anyway,
there's no time to stand here
gossiping." He fiddled with his
headset. "Ten seconds to broadcast!"

The *Stunt Mania!* theme tune blared out over the loudspeakers.

**Stunt Mania! Stunt Mania! Stunt Mania! Stunt MAY-NEE-ARRRRRR!**

As the tune crashed towards it's big finish, Jeremy looked at the Stunt Monkeys and winked.

"Credits rolling? OK people. Counting us in. Ten, nine, eight..."

From behind a screen the presenter, Simon Fudge-Smythe, stalked out fixing his hair. He scowled at the Stunt Monkeys and checked his microphone.

"Is this useless thing working? Am I the only professional in this excuse for a television station? I want to talk to my agent!"

"Seven, six..."

"Wait!" squeaked Einstein, but no one heard him (or, if they did, chose not to look like they had).

"Five, four..." Jeremy stopped counting and held up three fingers, then two, then one.

A camera whirled right up close to Simon Fudge-Smythe who switched on a beaming smile exactly as the red light on top of the camera went on. A sign at the back of the studio lit up: 'On Air'.

"HI!" yelled Simon at the camera. "Welcome to the very first edition of *Stunt Mania!* If, like me, you watched last year's SludgeFest 50 disaster and wondered just which masters of merriment could have caused such marvellous mayhem, then tonight's your lucky night! We tracked down the four TOTALLY KRAZEE boys behind the disaster, and in a couple of moments we'll be bringing them right into your living rooms!" Simon pointed at the boys.

"There'll be a chance to chat to the boys later, but right now let's 'dive' straight in and see these Stunt Monkeys do their stuff! What you are about to see is the first live televised attempt on the **World Record for Underwater Speed Piranha Rodeo**! It's all quite simple: the boys just have to transfer these 'super-friendly' Amazonian Bone-cutter piranhas as fast as they can from one tank to the other. Hopefully they can do it without losing too many fingers! The lovely Miss Axelsen from **The League of Unbelievable and Amazing World Records** is on hand to make sure everything is OK! That's all coming up after this commercial break!"

"Welcome back," smiled Simon as the advert ended. "The boys are in position and they're ready to do their stuff! Take it away boys!"

Both cameras swivelled round to point at the Stunt Monkeys, who stood blinking under the lights. There was a long, awkward silence. From his position behind the cameras, Jeremy pulled a strange face, and mouthed the words, "Do something NOW!"

Grunt glared straight at the camera.

Einstein folded his arms and pretended to inspect the fish tank.

Stench let out a small squeak of a fart.

STUNT
MONKEYS

Miss Axelsen, a fixed smile on her face, stood waiting for the Stunt Monkeys to do something.

Offscreen, Jeremy was silently imitating a man swallowing a whole pineapple. Only Kurtis seemed to realize they were on TELEVISION. He grabbed hold of Stench and pulled him up the ladder.

"There they go folks!" yelped Simon with some relief. His voice lowered to a whisper as tense drumming music started up in the background. "Inside that specially reinforced fish tank is 60,000 litres of pure Amazonian river water packed with one thousand vicious Amazonian Bone-cutter piranhas just waiting to see where their next meal is coming from! Bone-cutters can eat an entire bulldozer in less than eight seconds! Just imagine what they could do to these four brave, but extremely foolish, boys! What don't we do studio audience?"

"WE DON'T TRY THIS AT HOME!" roared the crowd of old age

pensioners, chubby grannies and batty retired colonels who made up the studio audience.

Einstein went even paler than usual. Grunt shrugged his shoulders and scooted up the ladder behind Kurtis.

"What's the plan, chief?" whispered Grunt, grinning like a maniac.

Kurtis was smiling for the cameras, too.

"Haven't got a stuffin' clue," he whispered from between his teeth. "I was kind of hoping you'd come up with something."

"Einstein!" hissed Grunt. "Any bright ideas?"

But before Einstein could come up with a bright idea (which was just as well because Einstein didn't actually have one), Stench stripped down to his grimy underpants, took a deep breath and dived into the piranha-infested tank.

"Oh my gosh!" yelped Simon. "Stinky boy has gone in viewers! I can hardly watch!"

The Bone-cutters paused for a second, and then headed straight for Stench hardly believing their luck that someone had been dumb enough to leap into their tank.

Dinner time.

The piranhas swarmed towards Stench, their teeth snapping like castanets. At the very last second, Stench screwed up his face and a super-powered jetstream of fart bubbles shot out of his rear end. Instantly, he took off like a rocket, careering around the tank in tight circles. Seconds later, a column of water began to form inside the centre of the tank.

"He's creating a whirlpool!" shouted Einstein, dashing up the ladder.

"C'mon," said Kurtis and leaped
in, quickly followed by Grunt.
Stench, his bottom a blur of bubbles,
zoomed past them.

The piranhas were
being swished round
and round so quickly
that, one by one,
they began to faint.
As they fainted,
Grunt and Kurtis
hoicked them out
and threw them
to Einstein, who
lobbed them
into the second
tank. With a final
burst of fart
power, Stench

launched himself clear of the tank. He landed with a splash in the second tank, the last dozen fish trailing behind him like the tail of a kite.

"1000! 1000! 1000!" As the large red piranha-counting display unit flashed on and off, Stench scrambled out of the tank.*

"How did they do, Miss Axelsen? Do we have a new World Record?" said Simon, his eyes bulging with excitement.

Miss Axelsen checked her stopwatch. She turned to Simon.

"One thousand piranhas transferred in just one minute twenty three seconds. I can confirm that's an official **League of Unbelievable and Amazing World Record for Underwater Speed Piranha Rodeo!** Well done, Stunt Monkeys!"

"Stunt-tastic!" screamed Simon

Fudge-Smythe. "Totally stunt-tastic!"

Jeremy Smashing grinned and hugged his clipboard.

*Stunt Mania!* was going to be a hit!

*No piranhas were harmed during the writing of this scene.

# CHAPTER
## FOUR

### McFOODLE RETURNS

Outside Channel Sludge, the fully
recovered Mayor McFoodle sat
watching the show from inside a
Sludgeville Grass Inspection van
parked up against the studio wall.
He was flanked by Assistant Pink
and two lines of black-clad Grass
Inspectors. Only their flinty eyes

showed through the slits in their balaclavas.

"This is it men," said Mayor McFoodle. "Our chance to catch these horrid little squits red-handed! They're in there right now showing off on live TV, and almost certainly breaking lots and lots of rules! No mercy is to be shown! I want them bagged, tagged and, and, um – oh you know what I mean! Just get them!"

Assistant Pink flung open the back of the van and the Grass Inspection team crashed into Studio 7, followed by a puffing McFoodle.

He charged into the glare of the studio lights and pulled out his Mayor badge.

"STOP RIGHT THERE!" he yelled triumphantly. "NO ONE MOVE! THIS IS AN OFFICIAL SLUDGEVILLE COUNCIL, er, GRASS INSPECTION."

There was total silence.

The Mayor, Assistant Pink and the Grass Inspectors shaded their eyes and stared.

Studio 7 was completely empty.

"But, but, but," said Mayor McFoodle, "I just saw them on TV!"

A man wearing overalls and carrying a broom walked by.

"You there!" shouted Mayor McFoodle. "Man with broom! What's the meaning of this? Why is the studio empty? Where are those blasted Stunt Monkeys?"

The man with the broom stopped and looked at him.

"They've gone," he said. "Gone 'ome."

"But we were just watching them!" said Mayor McFoodle, making the shape of a TV with his fingers in case the broom man didn't understand what a television was.

"The. Show. Was. Recorded," said the broom man as if talking to a chimpanzee.

"That's right," said a voice from the darkness. "We wouldn't risk four boys being eaten on live television. That wouldn't do at all. No, we record it so if they do get eaten we can edit it out. You see? Simple really, once it's explained in words. Love the chain by the way, very bling."

Jeremy Smashing came forward out of the shadows, startling one of the Grass Inspectors who dropped into a fighting stance and shrieked a ninja death scream at the top of his voice.

"Careful mate!" said the chief Grass Inspector. "He could have 'ad your arm off then, sneakin' up like that! He's a trained killer!"

"Good for him," said Jeremy. "Now, who are you people and what are you doing in my studio?"

Mayor McFoodle drew himself up to his full height and looked up at Jeremy.

"Everyone knows who I am! I am The Honourable Mayor Horace T. McFoodle!"

"You could be The Lord of the Rings for all I know," sniffed Jeremy. "I only moved to Sludgeville a few months ago. I don't think I've heard about any mayor. Where've you been hiding all this time?"

"I ... I ..." spluttered the Mayor.

"His Excellency the Mayor has been temporarily indisposed," said Pink, stepping forward. "But now he's back ... and he'd like to know exactly where those four boys are. They are fugitives from justice!"

"Really?" said Jeremy. "That's most odd because I have a piece of

paper in my office from the Grotburg County Court which tells me they are no longer fugitives from justice."

Mayor McFoodle shook with anger. "Well they soon will be! And I demand that you tell me their exact location right this minute!"

"Don't get in a snit. It's simple to find out where they are, and I suppose you'll find out soon enough," said Jeremy flicking on a nearby TV screen. "They're famous! They've got their own 24-hour TV channel!"

Mayor McFoodle watched, horrified, as the Stunt Monkeys 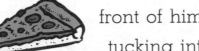 appeared on the screen in front of him. They were tucking into a huge pizza as they discussed their stunt for the following week.

"You mean there's going to be more of this jiggery-pokery going on?" he asked Jeremy.

Jeremy looked at him.

"Of course there's going to be more! This is going to be huge! With a bit of luck this show will run for years! As long as the audience figures keep going up we'll keep showing *Stunt Mania!*. This is television! It's what we do. Now, if

you don't mind, I'm a very busy man, so can you get your pet bananas in pyjamas out of my studio?"

He pointed at the Grass Inspectors and, turning his back on Mayor McFoodle, marched off.

Mayor McFoodle looked up at the TV screen.

"You heard what he said, Pink? This could be going on for years!"

Assistant Pink pursed his lips. "It doesn't bear thinking about, sir."

"That's right, Pink!" snarled the Mayor. "Which is exactly why we're going to put an end to all this nonsense once and for all!"

# CHAPTER FIVE

## FAME

It was the day after the first *Stunt Mania!* show and the boys were in Stench's back garden, trying out some new ideas for next week's show. Grunt stretched a final elastic band around Einstein, whose crash-helmeted head was sticking out of what looked like a giant rubber ball.

He rocked back and forth.

"What do you think?" said Grunt.

Kurtis glanced up from his sketch pad in which he'd been writing new ideas. "What is it?"

Grunt started to bounce Einstein like a basketball.

"Hey!" said Einstein. "You didn't say anything about bouncing!"

**"World Record for a Human Basketball!"** said Grunt. "I thought I explained?"

He bounced Einstein towards a large hoop he'd made out of an old wire coat hanger and attached to Stench's garden fence.

He took aim and then shot Einstein high into the air...

...and through the hoop.

"AAAARGH!"
yelled Einstein.

"He shoots, he
scores!" cried Grunt.

Einstein bounced on to the
lawnmower and slammed straight
into the Channel Sludge
cameraman, who fell to the ground,
only just saving his camera.

"Needs work," said Kurtis. "But it
does give me an idea."

He scribbled a few notes on his
sketch pad.

"I'll just give it a few more tries,"
said Grunt, walking across to
Einstein. "Maybe I need to drop him
from a ladder, get a bigger bounce?"

"No!" yelled Einstein. "Get me out
of this! I never should have..."

But before Einstein could
finish, Stench, a cloth tied
tightly around his eyes,
whooshed by on a cloud
of fart holding a
stopwatch in his
hand. The TV
crew reached
for their back
pockets and quickly rammed
clothes pegs on to their noses.
A week with Stench had taught them
to be prepared.

"Let me guess..." said Kurtis, with
a grin. "...World Record for Blindfold
Speed Farting?"

Stench nodded and careered straight into the garden shed. Kurtis winced and went over to check that Stench wasn't too badly hurt.

"I think we need to look at my idea," he said, picking up his sketch pad. "Board meeting in two minutes!"

It took more than two minutes to untangle Einstein from the elastic bands, but before too long the Stunt Monkeys were sitting in Stench's bedroom waiting to hear Kurtis's big idea.

"What's with the sunglasses, Einstein?" asked Grunt from his comfy position on Stench's bedroom

floor. "You going to the beach or something?"

Einstein scowled at Grunt, pushed his fancy new sunglasses up his nose and moved carefully past Stench, who was busy signing a large stack of glossy photos of himself tackling the piranhas from last week's show. Tim, Stench's pet vulture, peered down from his usual perch on top of the wardrobe where he'd built a nest out of old pizza boxes and boxer shorts. He was eating a steak that a fan had sent in after hearing that Stench fed him on roadkill.

# Tim's Top Training Tips!

If you're thinking of getting a pet vulture like Stench, remember that

## A vulture is for life, not just for Christmas!

If you do decide to go ahead you'll need to make sure it's properly fed.

### Training Tip 1:

Feeding pet vultures can be difficult and expensive. Personally I'd prefer to be fed on rare French steak, but Stench cuts down on cost by scooping up roadkill. I guess I'm not that fussy – hey, I'm a vulture, remember, I like dead animals!

Collect all of Tim's Top **Training Tips** and have a happy vulture of your own!

"So are you going to the beach?" Grunt persisted.

"No," said Einstein. "They're just..."

"Just what?" said Kurtis.

"Well ... just because we're stars now, aren't we? And big TV stars wear sunglasses at all times! In fact I think the rest of you guys should start wearing some. Ouch!" Einstein banged into the cameraman, who had been pointing the lens right into his face.

"You dipstick!" Grunt laughed. "You can't even see where you're going! 'TV star' my—"

"The TV crew are starting to really bug me," interrupted Einstein, rubbing his knee. "First they filmed me in my pants, then they interviewed my mum, and this morning they followed me into the bathroom!"

"Wait until they follow Stench into the bathroom," said Kurtis. "That might make them a bit less keen."

Stench dropped a particularly smelly one and smiled at the cameraman. The cameraman, as usual, didn't say a word.

"And that's another thing," said Grunt. "I hate the way these blokes

**68**

never say anything! They're like a Stenchy fart in a crowded lift – silent and annoying."

"Why can't you say anything?" Kurtis asked the sound man. The sound man just shrugged. Grunt dropped to the floor and bit him on the kneecap.

"OW!" yelped the sound man. "What was that for?"

"So you can talk?" said Kurtis.

"Of course I can talk. We're just not allowed to," said the sound man, rubbing his knee. "It's reality TV. If the audience knew we were here it'd spoil it, right?"

Kurtis sighed. Having the cameras around all the time was the only bad thing about *Stunt Mania!*. Everything else was great – and best of all, they were being paid to do whatever crazy stunts they liked on TV!

"Let's get down to business," said Kurtis. "After that fish thing we need to come up with something really good for the next show."

"Just wait a second, Kurtis," said Grunt. He stood up, walked over to Stench's wardrobe and opened the door. "There's something really interesting in here I want to show you all. Come and take a look."

The TV crew barged their way over to the wardrobe.

"Just in there," said Grunt. The
crew leaned forwards and, with
a firm shove, Grunt pushed
them inside and
locked the door.

"What are you
doing?" said
Einstein.

"If we're going to
talk about next week's
stunt we don't want the cameras on
us, do we? Jeremy said McFoodle
had been sniffing around the studio.
If he finds out what our next stunt is,
he's bound to try and stop us. And
that's the last thing we need, right?"

Kurtis nodded.

"Good thinking, Grunt." He glanced

at the wardrobe. "We'll let them out when we've finished. Now, see what you think of this."

He opened up his sketch pad and the others gathered round.

Kurtis pointed to a picture of a  man wearing a white spangly suit and sitting on a huge motorbike.

"This guy tried to jump across the Grand Canyon on a rocket-powered motorbike! How about we try something like that right here in Sludgeville? Just imagine jumping Sludgeville Gorge! Only not on a motorbike ... we can use a rocket-powered golf cart!"

He sat back and beamed.

"Awesome!" said Grunt.

"What happened to him?" said Einstein. "The guy on the rocket-powered motorbike."

"Well, he, erm ... crashed," said Kurtis. "But that doesn't mean we will!"

Einstein didn't look convinced, although as he was still wearing his fancy sunglasses it was hard to tell.

"What do you reckon, Stench?" said Grunt. "This gorge jump a go-er?"

Stench nodded his head and gave the thumbs up.

"Well that's it then," said Kurtis. "Next stop Sludgeville Gorge!"

# CHAPTER SIX

## STUNT MONKEYS ARE GO!

The rest of that week passed quickly.
The boys were interviewed by all
the press. Kurtis appeared on a TV
chat show. Grunt advertised a
laxative chocolate. Einstein was
featured on the cover of *Inventions
and Inventors* and Stench did a
fashion shoot for *Pig Farming Monthly*.

McFoodle was nowhere to be seen.

"I don't like it," said Kurtis. "McFoodle's being too quiet."

"Who cares?" said Grunt. "He's probably watching our highlights!"

Oddly enough, that was exactly what Mayor McFoodle was doing. In his office at Sludgeville Town Hall he sat in front of a large TV, his finger on a remote, watching a video of the Stunt Monkeys in Stench's back garden. Mayor McFoodle wound the tape forwards and then backwards.

"Look!" he said as he inched the tape forward frame by frame. The camera tracked Stench as he flew past Kurtis, and for a split second, Kurtis's sketch pad flashed into view.

Mayor McFoodle paused the tape and tilted his head. Assistant Pink did the same.

"Well, well, well," said Mayor McFoodle, smiling. "So that's your little game, is it?"

By the time Friday afternoon came, there was still no sign of McFoodle, and the Stunt Monkeys forgot all about him as they prepared to record the stunt for the Saturday

night *Stunt Mania!* show.

"But isn't this, like, completely, totally, amazingly, UNBELIEVABLY dangerous?" said Einstein, looking at the set builders putting the finishing touches to the long steep ramp on the edge of a cliff.

"Of course it's dangerous you muppet," said Grunt. "We're going to try and jump Sludgeville Gorge in a rocket-powered golf cart. It's supposed to be dangerous."

Einstein looked across the gorge, which stretched out between cliffs rising from the River Sludge. The whole thing looked much bigger than when they'd been discussing it back in Stench's bedroom.

"And remind me why we're using a golf cart?" said Einstein.

"The World Record. No one else has jumped Sludgeville Gorge in a rocket-powered golf cart before. And don't worry about crashing too much; we'll be wearing these. Show 'em, Stench."

Stench pulled a strange-looking rubbery item of clothing from a box and put it on.

"Came up with the idea after watching Grunt's basketball stunt," said Kurtis. "I had the TV props department make them. They're self-inflating safety suits. Sort of like personal airbags. Watch."

Kurtis pushed Stench over.

Before he hit the
ground the safety suit
inflated at a super-
fast speed and Stench
bounced harmlessly, like a
smelly beach ball.

"Excellent!" said Grunt.

Jeremy Smashing appeared at the
wheel of his personalized golf cart.
"How's it all going? Everything
ticketyboo?"

Everything was indeed ticketyboo.

The ramp was completed, as was
the landing strip on the far side of
the gorge. Miss Axelsen from **The
League of Unbelievable and Amazing
World Records** was standing by,
stopwatch and clipboard in hand.

The Stunt Monkeys put on their safety suits and headed for their rocket-powered golf cart, which was packed with NASA-grade jet fuel.

It was time to break the **World Record for Jumping Sludgeville Gorge in a Rocket-Powered Golf Cart.**

Grunt sat behind the wheel, Kurtis beside him, with Stench and Einstein in the back. As well as their special safety suits, they all wore super-strong crash helmets. Still, as they looked down the steep ramp, even Grunt had to admit it looked pretty hairy.

Jeremy Smashing leaned in and smiled encouragingly.

"All set to make television history? Jolly good. Now, if – sorry, I mean when – when you get across to the other side Simon will be there to interview the survivors. Sorry! Just my little joke. I'm sure it'll all be fine. Just tell him how thrilling it all was."

"I dunno about this," said Einstein. "We're strapped into a golf cart!"

"With a massive rocket on it," pointed out Grunt.

"That doesn't make me feel any better. Don't rockets, like, explode?"

"Parp!" Stench farted impatiently.

"Stench is right! What are we waiting for? Let's do it!" said Kurtis. "Pedal to the metal! Stunt Monkeys are go!"

Grunt pressed the golf cart's ignition switch and the rocket burst into life. The cameramen who'd been filming close-ups nervously backed away as the golf cart shook with power. A gigantic plume of flame and smoke shot out from behind the cart.

# STUNT MONKEYS

Grunt looked at the rest of the
Stunt Monkeys, gave the thumbs up,
and pressed the accelerator pedal.
The cart paused for a micro-second,
and then, with a mighty roar,
zoomed headfirst down the
ramp straight towards
Sludgeville Gorge.

WHOOOOOOSSSSSHHHH!!!!!!

It hit the upturn at a jillion kilometres an hour.

"Aiiiiieeeee!" screamed Einstein.

"Whoo-hoooooo!" yelled Grunt.

"Yeee-ha!!" whooped Kurtis, who'd been watching a cowboy movie the night before.

"PARP!" Stench's bottom made the loudest noise of all as the golf cart left the ramp and launched itself into the air, flames trailing from its rear end.

"We're gonna make it!" shouted Kurtis as they reached halfway.

Just then, a beeping sound started on the special control panel Channel Sludge had installed to check the golf cart during its flight. On Kurtis's headset Jeremy's crackly voice came through.

"I don't know – chzz – quite how to tell you this boys but, um, it seems you've got an extra passenger – crackle."

Kurtis took a quick look around the golf cart, but apart from the beeping sound, couldn't find a thing out of place. There certainly wasn't anyone there who shouldn't have been.

"Negative Jeremy, everything here is fi—"

Before he could finish, the golf

cart gave a shudder. There was a bang and a face appeared dangling from the roof. The face was upside down and getting blown about by the wind, but there was no mistaking who it was.

It was Mayor McFoodle and he was carrying a large rule book.

"You!" shouted Grunt.

"Yes me! The Honourable Mayor Horace T. McFoodle in person, and I order you under emergency council powers granted me in an emergency super-secret council meeting this afternoon," he held up the rule book, his eyes gleaming strangely, "to stop this golf cart immediately!"

"But why didn't you try and stop us before we took off?" said Einstein. "And how come we didn't see you?"

"Before take-off I concealed myself in the drinks box. As for why I didn't stop you before take-off, although I can't stop you performing your little stunts on the ground, I can as soon as you're airbourne under **Emergency Rule 203a (subsection 3):** No operating an airline without the correct licence. And I've caught you red-handed! Now stop this plane!"

"Plane?" said Kurtis. "This isn't a plane! It's a golf cart!"

"It's flying, isn't it?" said the Mayor. "It's got passengers, hasn't it? That's close enough for me!"

The Stunt Monkeys were about to argue some more when something came up.

The ground.

The golf cart hit the landing strip with an almighty bang. All four safety suits inflated at once, and the Stunt Monkeys bounced clear. Mayor McFoodle fell into the driving seat and grabbed the wheel, but his short legs were unable to reach the brake pedal and the cart careered straight

towards Simon Fudge-Smythe.

Simon, a fixed TV smile on his face, realized too late that the golf cart wasn't going to stop in time.

"Erk!" he cried as it knocked him and his perfect teeth high up into the air, and, "Noooo!" as he came down to land in the Sludgeville Sewage Treatment Plant on a bed of poo.

McFoodle and the golf cart zipped right through the landing strip and on to Sludgeville High Street, smashing into the Town Hall with an almighty wallop. The Mayor somersaulted out of the cart right through his office window, and landed, upside down, on his chair behind his desk.

Assistant Pink, who had been cleaning the filing cabinet with a toothbrush, leaped into the air in surprise.

"Ah, Pink," said Mayor McFoodle. "There you are."

# CHAPTER
## SEVEN

### IT'S FOR YOU!

Mayor McFoodle slumped back in his chair, drumming his fingers on the desk.

"It's no good, Pink. I think I've lost the will to boss people around. If I can't manage to stop those stupid boys I might as well stop being mayor and go back to being plain

old MISTER Horace T. McFoodle."

Pink shuddered.

"Oh no, Your Magnificence! You can't think that way! You were born to boss people around! And Sludgeville needs you! Now more than ever!"

Mayor McFoodle was about to say something, when the phone rang.

Assistant Pink picked it up. "Mayor McFoodle's office, Assistant Pink speaking." He listened to the voice at the end of the line before covering the mouthpiece.

"It's Miss Axelsen from **The League of Unbelievable and Amazing World Records** for you, Your Worship."

He passed the phone over.

"Mayor McFoodle speaking," he said.

"Congratulations!" trilled Miss Axelsen. "I'm calling to let you know that you are now the official holder of the **World Record for Jumping Sludgeville Gorge in a Rocket-Powered Golf Cart!**"

"What!" yelped Mayor McFoodle. "There must be some mistake!"

"Absolutely not," said Miss Axelsen, "I was there and I saw the whole thing."

"B ... b ... but, that ridiculous stunt was nothing to do with me."

"I know you weren't officially on the list of participants," said Miss Axelsen, "but the fact is that you did jump Sludgeville Gorge and you did it in a rocket-powered golf cart. Of course, you do share the record with the Stunt Monkeys. We'll need your picture for the book..."

Miss Axelsen was still chattering away as Mayor McFoodle handed the phone back to Assistant Pink. He slumped further into his chair, a defeated look on his face.

The phone rang again, and the Mayor snatched it up.

"What now, you stupid woman?" he barked. "Miss Axelsen? Miss Axelsen?"

Mayor McFoodle gazed at the phone in his hand, a puzzled look on his face.

"Pink," he said. "Why is the phone still ringing when there's no one at the other end?" He stared at Pink. "What is it? You've gone very pale."

"The phone," said Pink. "That's not our normal phone."

Pink tapped a section of Mayor McFoodle's desk, and a panel slid back. A red telephone with a flashing light on top rose from inside the secret compartment.

Mayor McFoodle looked at it. "What's the meaning of this, Pink? Why is there a secret phone in my desk and how do you know about it?"

"It's the Emergency Mayor Phone," said Pink, who was still as white as an albino polar bear. His voice dropped to a whisper. "Lord Copperbottom had them installed when you were, um, indisposed."

Mayor McFoodle gasped. Lord Copperbottom!

Lord Copperbottom, or Lord Mayor Copperbottom of Belchtown, to give him his full title, had been the most-feared, chief boss mayor of all the mayors there had ever been in the entire history of mayoring ... until his untimely death.

The phone was still ringing.

"Well?" said Mayor McFoodle. "Are you going to answer it?"

Assistant Pink gingerly picked up the receiver.

"Mayor McFoodle's office. Assistant Pink speaking."

Pink listened.

"Yes," he said. And then "yes"
again. And then three more "yeses".
"Of course," said Pink. "Right away,
sir!" He put down the phone.

"Well?" said Mayor McFoodle.
"Who was it?"

"It was Lord Copperbottom,"
stammered Pink.

"But Copperbottom's dead, isn't
he?" said Mayor McFoodle,
anxiously. "Fell into the parking fine
offenders tarpit."

"That was the official story, Your
Highness, yes. However, while you
were staying at Gentle Landings he
paid us a visit."

Pink shivered at the memory.

"He was very much alive and

kicking, Your Worship. And he wants to see you tonight. At Grimly Towers."

"Me?!" Mayor McFoodle had turned a ghostly white. "Tonight? Do I have to? Perhaps you should go instead?"

Assistant Pink shook his head.

"I'm not sure that would be a good idea, Your Magnificence. No one ever says 'no' to Lord Copperbottom."

It was almost dark, and a steady black rain fell from the heavy sky. Mayor McFoodle and Assistant Pink were in the most rundown area of Sludgeville. They stepped out of the council limo and stared up at a gigantic, crumbling office block.

"Grimly Towers?" said Mayor McFoodle. "Lord Copperbottom lives at Grimly Towers? I thought Sludgeville Council stopped work on Grimly years ago."

"They did, Your Highness. It's been condemned. But this is where he said we should come," said Pink, wrinkling his nose against the rain.

"Well, go on then. Lead the way!" said Mayor McFoodle.

Pink pushed open the creaking metal door and the two men disappeared inside the dark and spooky building.

"He said top floor," said Pink, producing a small torch from his pocket. "I hope the lift works."

It didn't.

"There's nothing for it, Pink," said Mayor McFoodle. "We'll have to walk."

Thirty minutes later they were almost at the top.

"C'mon, Pink," urged McFoodle.

"Floor 99. Only one more floor to go! Put some effort in man!"

"Yes, Your Magnificence," Pink puffed. "Perhaps if I could stop carrying you now? I'm quite tired."

"Tired, Pink? I'm the one carrying the blasted torch! Oh very well, put me down."

Pink sank to his knees gasping for breath.

Mayor McFoodle shone the torch up the last flight of stairs. At the top, a huge wooden door with iron handles barred the way.

Mayor McFoodle trembled.

"That looks pretty spooky! After you, Pink, just in case."

Pink nervously pushed open the door which let out a loud CREEEEEAAAAAK.

"Come," said a deep voice from inside.

Mayor McFoodle and Assistant Pink tiptoed into the room.

A huge figure wrapped in a black robe that hung down in inky tatters came slowly towards them, a heavy chain clanking around its neck.

"Lord Copperbottom!" gasped Mayor McFoodle.

"The very same," said Lord Copperbottom, his voice echoing in the darkness.

A lantern on the wall spread weak light around the room to reveal an office lined with dusty files and cabinets. On a desk was a gleaming computer and a telephone.

"Meased to pleet you, Your Worship, I mean pleased moo teet you, teased poo yeet mou," he stuttered. "Mayor Horace T. McFoodle at your service."

"I know who you are, McFoodle," said Lord Copperbottom. "You're that spineless excuse for a mayor who's letting a bunch of miserable little vermin run rings around you back in Sludgeville, aren't you?"

"I, well, that is, you see, um, erm, that is … um technically, I suppose, perhaps. Um, yes," burbled Mayor McFoodle.

Lord Copperbottom shot a disgusted look in the Mayor's direction and lit another lantern. He sat down on one side of the desk and pointed to a facing chair.

"Sit," he said to Mayor McFoodle, who sat like an obedient poodle.

"We simply can't have this, McFoodle," rumbled Lord Copperbottom. "Rules, good rules, being disobeyed here there and everywhere! What would happen to the reputation of councils up and down the land, hmm? Just imagine

if every scuttlebucket child decided to do whatever they liked – to have fun?"

He drummed his bony fingers on the desk and looked at Mayor McFoodle.

"I've called you in here today, McFoodle, for retraining."

Mayor McFoodle gulped. Retraining sounded scary.

Lord Copperbottom pressed a button on his desk. There was a soft hiss and a section of wall to his left slid back.

Inside was a gleaming laboratory. Wires and machinery hummed, and a man in a white lab coat sat at a computer keyboard. In the centre of the room was a large piece of equipment that looked a bit

like a mini-submarine.

"The Mayor Retraining and Refit Module," smiled Lord Copperbottom, revealing a row of tiny little shark-like teeth. "A quick spin in there should put you back on track in no time, McFoodle!"

"Pink!" squeaked Mayor McFoodle, leaping on to Assistant Pink's lap.

"I won't lie to you," said Lord Copperbottom. "This is going to hurt."

# CHAPTER EIGHT

## THERE'S *NO BUSINESS LIKE* SHOW BUSINESS

Channel Sludge got its best ratings ever for the Saturday show. Jeremy Smashing had made sure that a clip of Mayor McFoodle at the wheel of the golf cart had been shown in between other programmes. By the time *Stunt Mania!* aired everyone wanted to see what had happened.

The Stunt Monkeys were becoming even more famous. Other TV stations wanted interviews. All the newspaper reporters wanted to talk to them and everywhere they went people wanted to take photos. Stench had even found a photographer hiding under his bed.

There was only one problem. McFoodle.

"I wish he wouldn't keep sticking his miserable nose into things," said Grunt, as the boys headed into Channel Sludge for a meeting with Jeremy. "That man really bugs me."

Stench farted in agreement.

"We'll just have to be even more secretive next time," said Kurtis.

"That's not going to be so easy," said Einstein, glancing at the TV crew who, as always, were hovering around them like flies. "With these clowns filming everything, McFoodle can see every move we make."

"I'll see what I can come up with," said Kurtis as he opened the door to the meeting room, which was packed with *Stunt Mania!* crew.

"Hello boys!" trilled Jeremy Smashing. He held up the front page of the *Daily Sludge* which showed a large picture of the golf cart roaring across Sludgeville Gorge. "We've got an absolute smash on our hands! It's all so smashing!"

The Stunt Monkeys shooed away a

couple of Channel Sludge lawyers who had been inspecting each other's hair for insects, and sat down at the boardroom table.

"So," said Jeremy to the boys. "Any brilliant ideas for next week's show?"

"Something less dangerous," said Einstein.

Everyone laughed and Einstein looked puzzled.

Kurtis pushed up his sunglasses, leaned back in his chair and put his feet on the table.

"We were thinking of doing something that involved large amounts of mess, maybe breaking the **World Record for the Biggest Food Fight**, something along those lines," said Kurtis.

"Yeah!" said Grunt. "Make it really gungy! Get right up McFoodle's nose!"

Just then, the door flew open and Mayor McFoodle stormed in. Assistant Pink scurried in behind him, with six Ninja Traffic Wardens.

"Oh not you again," sighed
Jeremy. "I thought we'd been
through everything already?"

"Not quite everything, Mr Smashing," said Mayor McFoodle in an odd voice. "We have been looking at our rule book again and found that Channel Sludge has broken the **Sludgeville Council Anti-Fun Emergency Rule 45344444**: No boys are to appear on TV doing anything fun, exciting or otherwise remotely interesting anywhere within Sludgeville, from now until the end of time."

He passed a sheet of official Sludgeville Council paper to Jeremy, who looked at it and passed it to one of the Channel Sludge lawyers.

"Well?" said Jeremy. "Is he right?"

The lawyer nodded. "Looks watertight to me, boss. We're gonna

have to shut down production. At least until we can get a judge to take a look at it."

Mayor McFoodle folded his arms and grinned.

"Looks like that's the end of *Stunt Mania!*, Mr Smashing! Perhaps now you'll put some proper shows back on like *Cheese World* or *Celebrity Gardening* instead!"

Mayor McFoodle pointed at the Stunt Monkeys. "And if any of you so much as passes wind without permission – yes, that includes you, stinkboy – I'll come down on you like a ton of bricks! And believe me, you won't know what's hit you! Good day!"

He waddled out of the office, followed at a march by the Ninja Traffic Wardens and Assistant Pink.

"Well," said Jeremy. "Anyone got any bright ideas?"

Kurtis leaned forward.

"Funnily enough..."

# CHAPTER
## NINE

### GIRLS JUST WANNA HAVE FUN

It didn't take long for the Stunt Monkeys to gather all they needed to put Kurtis's cunning plan into action. First they persuaded Jeremy to make this week's show a live broadcast.

"If we're live, it cuts down on McFoodle's chances of stopping us," Kurtis explained.

Next, they managed to give the camera crew the slip, so as not to give Mayor McFoodle any clue about their plan.

Once they'd got rid of the cameras, they paid a visit to the wardrobe department at Channel Sludge.

The biggest problem was Grunt.

"Uh uh," he said, his arms folded across his chest. "No chance, no way, NO."

"Come on Grunt," said Kurtis. "It's the only way we're going to keep the show going. Don't you want to put one over on McFoodle?"

"And the next one's going to be very messy," said Einstein. "You wouldn't want to miss that, would you?"

Grunt looked at Stench.

"How about you Stenchy? You going to go for this one?"

Stench shrugged, nodded and farted.

Grunt sighed.

"All right, I'll do it," he said. "But if anyone so much as *smiles* I'm walking, right?"

Kurtis and Einstein smiled.

It was on.

"Another coconut macaroon, Mayor McFoodle?"

"Don't mind if I do, Mrs McFoodle, don't mind if I do."

Mrs McFoodle passed the plate of macaroons to Mayor McFoodle who sat back in his favourite chair and turned on the TV with a contented sigh. Horace McFoodle Junior, now fully recovered from his accidental balloon trip to North Korea, sat quietly arranging his *Cheeses of the World* cards in a leather album.

Cheeses of the World.
Collector's Card Number 23:

Danish Blue.
A fine tangy cheese easily
recognized by the distinctive
'blue' speckling which runs
through it. Enjoy with crackers,
grapes and a glass of
sparkling water.

"I expect they'll have put *Celebrity Grass Makeover* back on instead of that idiotic stunt show," said Mayor McFoodle.

"I expect so, dear," said Mrs McFoodle, who was knitting a new pair of underpants for Horace Junior.

Mayor McFoodle popped a macaroon into his mouth as the news finished.

The TV screen faded. Music played.

**129**

"That's not the music for *Celebrity Grass Makeover!*" said Mayor McFoodle, shifting uncomfortably in his comfy chair. "Not unless they've changed it." His eyes glowed an angry red.

They hadn't changed it. It wasn't *Celebrity Grass Makeover.*

It was *Stunt Mania!.*

As the grinning Simon Fudge-Smythe hobbled into view on a pair of crutches, Mayor McFoodle almost choked on his macaroon.

"What?! Who?! Wha-huh! The, the, the, the ... rule-breaking swines!" he yelled at the TV set. "How dare they? How dare they disregard my rules!"

"Welcome to a special LIVE edition of *Stunt Mania!*," said Simon Fudge-Smythe. "The fantastic TV show that you, lovely viewers, have made top of the ratings! Sadly, for reasons beyond our control, the Stunt Monkeys will not be able to complete any stunts tonight."

The studio audience booed.

Mayor McFoodle relaxed slightly.

"Wait, wait folks," said Simon, holding his hands up. "I know many of you will be disappointed not to see the fabulous Stunt Monkeys –

**Sludgeville Council Rule 45344444** has prevented the boys appearing. However, the rule doesn't say anything about girls! So, ladies and gentlemen, boys and girls, please welcome the magnificent, the wonderful Stunt Sistas!"

The camera swooped to Simon's left and four girls bounced onstage, waving at the cameras.

"If you're thinking there's something very familiar about the Stunt Sistas you'd be right, folks! They are in fact the actual twin sisters of our very own Sludgeville Stunt Monkeys! And here they are! Gruntilda, Kurstie, Einola and the one and only Stenchine!"

From the comfort of his armchair, Mayor McFoodle had turned a deep shade of purple. "I don't believe it!" he screamed at the television, as Kurstie, her long blonde curls flapping, stepped forward.

"Our stunt tonight," she said in a wispy, high-pitched voice, "is very dangerous and extremely silly."

Kurstie waved the other Stunt
Sistas forward. Gruntilda in
particular seemed to be in no hurry
for the cameras to get a close up.

"This is the stupidest
idea you've ever had!"
hissed Grunt, as the
Stunt Sistas took their
places. "This wig is
killing me! And if
anyone ever finds out
about me wearing a dress and
make-up on national TV, I'll—"

"Be quiet, Gruntilda," said Kurtis.
He pushed his own blonde wig back
a little and checked his skirt, which
kept bunching up around his legs.
Girls clothes were so difficult to wear.

"At least we can keep doing the show like this!" he whispered. "And get one over on McFoodle."

Simon hobbled forward into the spotlight. "Tonight's stunt is one of the most disgusting, strange and ridiculous stunts ever undertaken! And what's more, you are all going to be involved!"

"Whooo!" said the studio audience.

Simon turned to Kurtis. "Kurstie, can you tell us what **Unbelievable and Amazing World Record** you are going to break tonight?"

"Yes, Simon, I can," said Kurtis in his girly voice. "Tonight the Stunt Sistas are going to attempt the **World Record for Mass Barfing!**"

Kurtis had got the mass barfing idea from the time when some of the Stunt Monkey's racing snails turned up in Mrs McFoodle's salad during a

 posh mayoral dinner. Mrs McFoodle was about to bite into one of Chef Pierre's sausages when ... it moved.

Mrs McFoodle had screamed and barfed all over the table. Before too long everyone in the place was barfing all over everyone else.

Kurtis had never forgotten it. And this was the chance to recreate that magic moment in front of the cameras and, hopefully, break another Unbelievable and Amazing World Record!

The Stunt Sistas took their places. Miss Axelsen from **The League of Unbelievable and Amazing World Records**, wearing a special plastic anti-barf suit, gave them the thumbs up. A drum roll began. **The World Record for Mass Barfing** was on!

Back in the McFoodle house, Mayor McFoodle had seen enough.

# CHAPTER
## TEN

### IS IT A BIRD? IS IT A PLANE?

High above Sludgeville, a flaming comet streaked across the night sky, heading towards Channel Sludge. Only a keen-eyed aeroplane pilot would have noticed that the fireball wasn't, in fact, a comet at all...

Below, in Studio 7, Gruntilda stood in front of a gigantic vat of goo.

"Ladies and gentlemen," said Simon, holding a handkerchief over his nose. "Inside that vat is a mixture of fishguts, organic yoghurt, bean curd, kippers, rancid custard, onion and garlic sauce, chocolate covered locusts, marzipan, old school dinners and just about anything disgusting that the Stunt Sistas could find!"

Some of the audience were already looking a little green. Stench flew slowly around the studio on a cloud of fart gas, just to help things along.

Grunt dipped a large ladle into the mixture and raised it to his lips. Nearby, the rest of the Stunt Sistas began to sway gently from side to side, like a ship bobbing on the ocean. There were groans from the audience. Grunt opened his mouth and swallowed the noxious goo.

Instantly, about half the audience began to barf. Simon Fudge-Smythe took one look and barfed all over a studio assistant, who barfed all over a man from the make-up department.

Up in the director's box, Jeremy Smashing barfed all over the sound desk, whilst back on stage, a panic-stricken Miss Axelsen tried to stop herself from joining in. Smothered in her anti-barf suit, there was nowhere for the barf to go...

Just as it seemed that everyone who could barf was barfing there was a loud BANG! from overhead and the studio filled with smoke.

"What's happening?" squeaked Einstein clutching Kurtis's blouse. "Is it the end of the world?"

Kurtis shook his head and wiped a streak of barf from his mouth.

"Don't think so. But something's coming through the studio roof. Look!"

Einstein, Grunt and Stench peered up into the dark shadows. There was a whine like a jet engine beginning to shut down, and out of the swirling clouds came a pair of feet, trailing blue-white flames, which cut out as they touched the studio floor.

Up in the director's
box, Jeremy Smashing
was running around in
small circles. "Keep
the cameras rolling!"
he shouted between
barfs.

As the smoke began
to clear, a massive,
evil-looking, robotic
figure, stood tall and
menacing, silhouetted
against one of the
studio spotlights.
Little spikes of
light bounced
off his shining
bowler hat.

"Is that ... no, it can't be, can it?" Kurtis said. "Mayor McFoodle?"

"AFFIRMATIVE!" snarled the figure in a voice like thunder.

"That means 'yes'," Einstein explained to Grunt.

"I know what it means, you dipstick!" snarled Grunt.

Kurtis stared up at McFoodle. "He's wearing some sort of robotic suit!"

The others peered closer. Kurtis
was right. In the robo-suit McFoodle
stood about three metres high. The
suit's metallic skin gleamed and
flickered as electric currents pulsed
through it.

Stench parped. Grunt took a step
forward and then, thinking better of
it, a step back.

"Help!" said Einstein.

Mayor McFoodle thundered
towards the Stunt Sistas. "Hello girls."
He lifted his arm and pointed right
at them. "I've got
something for you!"

"Ohmigod!" Einstein ducked behind Grunt. "He's going to vaporize us with an evil death ray!"

"Negative," growled McFoodle. "Although that is something to be considered." He pulled out a book from inside his suit and opened it with a giant metal hand.

A rule book.

"This show is cancelled!" said Mayor McFoodle. "New rules apply!"

"I say!" said Jeremy Smashing, appearing onstage. "You can't just come in here, smashing all our expensive television equipment and threatening our stars!"

A laser ray shot out from Mayor McFoodle's robot eyes and picked

Jeremy up off the floor. He squealed, helpless in its grip as he rose high above the ground.

"Oh really?" boomed the Mayor. "And who's going to stop me?" he asked, dumping Jeremy upside down in a large wheelie bin.

Simon Fudge-Smythe threw himself to the floor in front of McFoodle.

"Please don't hurt me, Oh Mighty Super Being!" he squeaked. "And if you do, don't damage the face!"

Mayor McFoodle scooped him up and flicked him carelessly out of the window at the back of the studio.

A few Channel Sludge security guards moved forward, trying to look a lot braver than they felt. At once, a team of Ninja Traffic Wardens abseiled through the roof and started handing out parking tickets.

"Quick," whispered Kurtis to the others, "let's get out of here."

They had almost made it to the door when McFoodle noticed them.

"Not so fast, slimeballs!" he shouted. "Where do you think you're going?"

And with that, a super clingy net shot out from his wrist, engulfing the Stunt Monkeys. Mayor McFoodle lifted them high into the air and brought them up to his face.

"He's gonna eat us!" wailed Einstein, pushing Grunt forward.

"Take him! I'm too skinny! There's a bit more meat on his bones!"

"No one's eating anyone," said Kurtis, although he didn't look too convinced.

"Bring it on, you big lump!" snarled Grunt. "I'm goin' down fightin'!"

Stench said nothing, but it did get very smelly in the net.

With a sudden 'whoosh' of flame and smoke, McFoodle launched himself up and out through the hole in the roof, taking the Stunt Monkeys with him.

"Uh-oh," said Kurtis, looking down at Sludgeville whizzing by beneath them, "this doesn't look good."

Then suddenly everything went dark.

# CHAPTER ELEVEN

## DEAD LETTER OFFICE

It was still very dark.

"OW!" said Grunt. "That's my eye you idiot! Keep still!"

"Stench! That stinks!"

"Who's standing on my foot!"

"Quiet," said Kurtis. "Someone's coming." He tugged off his wig and girlie dress. Luckily he'd still got his

T-shirt and jeans on underneath. The others quickly followed suit.

There was a sound of a drawer being opened, and the boys felt themselves pulled forwards into the light. They blinked and stared.

The first thing they noticed was that they were all wedged tightly into what looked like a large file. The second thing was that the file was contained within an even larger filing cabinet. In front of them was Mayor McFoodle in his giant robotic suit, grinning at them like a mad person. A huge man wearing long black robes stood behind him. Assistant Pink stood at the door, an anxious look on his face.

**STUNT MONKEYS**

Kurtis strained his neck over the edge of the drawer. They were in what seemed like a large office lined with giant filing cabinets. He read some of the labels on the drawers: 'Late Library Books', 'Sunday Shoppers', 'Unpaid Parking Tickets'. Muffled noises and bangs came from several of them.

"Where are we?" said Einstein.

"You're in the Dead Letter Office," said Mayor McFoodle. "It's where we keep ... rulebreakers. People who don't cut their grass, or who don't pay their parking fines, or nasty little stunt boys, for example."

"Congratulations, McFoodle. You've done it at last," said Kurtis. "You've finally gone completely mad."

"Mad, am I? Is it madness to want everything to be neat? Is it madness to want the grass to measure less than eight centimetres? Is it madness to file every vile little rulebreaker safely away where we can keep an eye on them? Is it madness to EXPECT PERFECTION?"

"Um, er, yes," said Kurtis. "Locking

people up in filing cabinets is about
as nutty as it gets. And you won't get
away with this!"

Mayor McFoodle smiled. "No? Just
watch me!"

Before Kurtis could say another
word, the filing cabinet slammed shut.

"Capital display, McFoodle," said
Lord Copperbottom. "Now let's see if
we can do something about those
criminal dog walkers and people who
feed the ducks without permission!
I've got a couple of special filing
cabinets put aside for them!"

Inside their cabinet, the Stunt
Monkeys hung in silence.

"Well, this is weird," said Grunt.
"I've never been filed before.

Not that I can remember, anyway. I think I would have remembered."

"Never mind that," said Kurtis. "Can anyone move? We've got to do something about McFoodle before he files everyone in Sludgeville!"

The boys wriggled around furiously, but it was no good. They were well and truly filed. From outside came the sound of footsteps.

"Oh no!" squeaked Einstein. "They're coming back to eat us!"

The drawer was pulled open again, and Assistant Pink leaned in. He looked around nervously.

"What do you want?" said Grunt. "Come to poke us with a sharp stick or something?"

"Quiet!" hissed Pink. "They'll hear you!"

He pressed a button, and a piece of machinery that looked like a giant claw appeared above the cabinet and lifted the Stunt Monkeys out. It lowered them to the floor, where they gratefully stretched their aching limbs. It had been very cramped inside. Not to mention smelly.

"I don't understand," said Kurtis.

"Why are you helping us?"

Assistant Pink looked around and fiddled with his tie.

"It's all gone too far!" he whispered. "Copperbottom is out of control. I don't like this new Mayor McFoodle and his robotic suit! I want the old macaroon-munching Mayor McFoodle back! I knew where we were with the old Mayor. It was a happy life helping to boss people around, but I think filing everyone in Sludgeville is too much!"

"You don't say?" said Kurtis.

"But why get us out?" said Einstein.

"Because you're the only ones stupid enough to try and stop them! Sludgeville needs you!"

# CHAPTER TWELVE

## DJ EMERGENCY

"I'm not sure I really want to save Sludgeville," said Grunt. "Maybe we should just leave Sludgeville to McFoodle and Copperbottom."

"No," said Kurtis, "Sludgeville may be a completely dull hole of unspeakable rubbishosity, but it's our completely dull hole of unspeakable

rubbishosity! It's our hometown! And this is our chance to get back at McFoodle for ruining *Stunt Mania!*."

"You're wasting time," said Pink. He led them up on to the roof. "Look!"

The Stunt Monkeys looked.

Far below, Sludgeville was being filed. The giant Mayor McFoodle could be seen scooping up wrongdoers and tossing them into a large box file. The Ninja Traffic Wardens hurried

after the Mayor, blasting every car
that wasn't parked properly, and the
Grass Inspectors dashed from house
to house, checking the length of
people's lawns using infra-red grass
length detector beams.

"TOO LONG!" they barked,
blowing up each and every lawn as
they moved down the street.

Everywhere the Stunt Monkeys
looked they could see burning cars,
blasted lawns and Sludgevillians
running for their lives.

"RULES ARE RULES!" screamed Mayor McFoodle. "CUT YOUR GRASS OR FACE THE WRATH OF ERM ... ME! OBEY PARKING RESTRICTIONS!" he howled, as yet another parked car bit the dust.

Mayor McFoodle lifted his giant robotic foot and booted the Sludgeville Youth Club. "THIS BUILDING DID NOT MEET COUNCIL APPROVAL. DESTROY! DESTROY!"

"Do you see?" said Assistant Pink. "He's changed!"

"No kidding, Sherlock," said Grunt.

"No, I mean Lord Copperbottom put him into some kind of retraining machine right here in Grimly Towers,

and this is what he ended up like! I don't just mean the new robotic suit – I mean he's really changed. I think his brain's been rewired!"

"That's it," said Kurtis. "We've got to get him back into that retraining machine and return him to normal!"

"Oh well," said Einstein, "no problem then. What do you think we should do; send him an invitation?"

Kurtis's eyes lit up. "Actually, Einstein, that's exactly what I think we should do!"

The others stared at him.

"What are you waiting for?" said Kurtis. "This is an emergency! Get me a mobile disco!"

# CHAPTER THIRTEEN

## A DJ SAVED MY LIFE

There was a short delay while the Stunt Monkeys checked that Kurtis hadn't been bumped on the head whilst inside the filing cabinet.

"There's nothing wrong with me!" snarled Kurtis, "I just need a mobile disco, you know, a DJ!"

Grunt shrugged and looked at

Einstein and Stench. "You heard.
Let's get him a DJ."

Fortunately, it turned out that one
of the filing cabinets inside Lord
Copperbottom's office contained
Darren Fishwick, better known in
Sludgeville as DJ Spanner*.

In less time than
it takes to say
'boogie', Darren
– a toilet
attendant by
day – had
transformed into DJ
Spanner, by the addition of
sunglasses and a spangly shirt.
While he zipped off to collect his
equipment, the Stunt Monkeys freed

*Need some WICKED CHOONS
at your wedding?
Some BANGING BEATS
at your bar mitzvah?
Just send for roadside assistance
from DJ SPANNER and his
MOBILE MUSICAL TOOL BOX!

everyone else who'd been
imprisoned in the filing cabinets,
including Jeremy Smashing, and
Miss Axelsen, who'd been filed for
putting Mayor McFoodle into **The
Book of Unbelievable and Amazing
World Records**.

"Quick!" said Kurtis. "To the roof!"
As everyone made their
way to the top of Grimly
Towers, DJ Spanner
arrived back, carrying
his decks and
speakers. In a flash, it
was all assembled.
"Any requests?"
"Just hit it!"
screamed Kurtis.

DJ Spanner twiddled some knobs
and music boomed out across
Sludgeville.

"OK everyone!" he yelled. "Great
to be here in Sludgeville! We're
gonna have a top night tonight! So
let's get down and boogie."

"Boogie!" Einstein repeated. "You
want us to dance?"

"Yes, Einstein, I want you to dance,"
cried Kurtis. "So get moving!" He
grabbed the mic. "Everyone dance!
Sludgeville needs you to dance!"

Slowly everyone began to dance.
Even old people. It was a truly
horrible sight.

Grunt twirled a finger next to his
head and rolled his eyes. "You know,

Kurtis, there's a time and a place for everything, and now is not the time to have a disco!"

"You think?" said Kurtis pointing down at Sludgeville. "I'd say there's never been a better time!"

Down in the part-ruined town, Mayor McFoodle looked up. The top of Grimly Towers was rocking. Disgusting music was booming out across Sludgeville in clear breach of a bazillion council rules.

Boogieing was taking place!

"Well, McFoodle?" yelled Lord Copperbottom, who had been supervising the Mayor's activities. "Are you going to let them get away with that horrible racket?"

Mayor McFoodle howled in anger.

He put down some people who hadn't spaced their flowers out properly and started towards Grimly Towers. Kurtis grabbed hold of Grunt and whispered something. Grunt grinned and, using a handy Sludgeville Council flag as a parachute, leaped straight off the side of Grimly Towers.

"I'll be back!" yelled Grunt, as he disappeared from view.

"It's working!" said Einstein, who had finally figured out what Kurtis was doing. "He's coming!"

Then he thought of something.

"What do we do when he gets here?"

Kurtis glanced over the side of the building. He saw Grunt land and run in the direction of Channel Sludge.

"We need to keep McFoodle busy for a moment or two," he said. "At least until Grunt gets back."

Einstein sighed. "We're all going to die."

"They're coming!" yelled Jeremy Smashing, beginning to film as the robot mayor started to climb up the outside of Grimly Towers, carrying Lord

Copperbottom in one hand.

On top of Grimly Towers, Simon Fudge-Smythe, a serious expression on his face, was talking into the camera.

"You're joining me, Simon Fudge-Smythe, live from Grimly Towers in Sludgeville, where a crazed Mayor McFoodle is—"

As McFoodle approached the top of Grimly Towers, one or two of the dancers began to look a bit nervous.

"Keep dancing!" yelled

Kurtis. "We need him up here in the open! I'll be back in a minute."

"Where are you going?" yelled Einstein.

"Just stall him!" shouted Kurtis, as he disappeared from view.

"Oh thanks," said Einstein. "And how do you suggest I do that? Ask him for a dance?"

Stench farted noisily.

McFoodle clambered over the edge of the tower block and stood facing the Sludgevillians.

"STOP THAT INFERNAL NOISE!" roared Mayor McFoodle, lifting his laser death ray thing and pointing it at the disco. DJ Spanner squeezed his eyes shut and started gibbering.

"Oh, save me, Mr Mayor, I promise—"

"DO IT!" yelled Copperbottom. "VAPORIZE THE DJ!"

Mayor McFoodle took aim.

"I can't look," cried Einstein, and buried his face in Stench's shoulder.

Just then, two things happened. There was a deafening roar and Grunt appeared, hovering in mid-air at the wheel of the rocket-powered golf cart.

Then Kurtis reappeared, clutching a massive reel of council red tape that he'd found in Lord Copperbottom's office. He tied one end to a concrete post and handed the other end to Stench.

"You know what to do, Stenchy?" said Kurtis.

Stench saluted, screwed up his face and, with a rip-roaring fart, launched himself towards the golf cart. The blowback hit Lord Copperbottom full in the face and he was blasted straight over the edge of Grimly Towers.

He screeched all the way down to the Sludgeville Toxic Waste Disposal Dump, and splashed into a vat of foul gunk.

Meanwhile, Mayor McFoodle was blasting at Grunt with all the weapons at his disposal. He didn't notice Stench weave his way expertly between the balls of flame and laser rays and land safely in the golf cart.

"Welcome aboard!" yelled Grunt.
"Phew-ee! That was a close one!"

He gunned the golf cart into a dive
and looped behind McFoodle, while
Stench fixed the tape to the cart.

"OK, party over! Everyone off the
roof!" yelled Kurtis. The crowd didn't
need telling twice. They dashed
down the one hundred flights of
stairs, and scattered in all directions.
Grunt and Stench circled the Mayor.
Round and round they flew, wrapping
the tape around him ever tighter.

"Are you getting all this?" yelled
Simon Fudge-Smythe into the
camera. He was almost underneath
McFoodle, who was hell bent on
shooting down the golf cart.

"This is great stuff!" yelled Jeremy Smashing, just as Simon Fudge-Smythe was knocked off the roof by a blow from Mayor McFoodle's foot.

"Nooo," he cried, as he too plunged towards the Sludgeville Toxic Waste Disposal Dump. "This is Simon Fudge-Smythe for Channel Sludge plunging into a giant vat of toxic slime."

By now, the red tape had wound itself around Mayor McFoodle so tightly he looked like a giant red Egyptian mummy. He couldn't move.

Grunt landed the golf cart on the roof, and switched off the engine. Miss Axelsen, who'd been hiding behind a disused air-conditioning unit, stepped forward.

"Congratulations boys!" she said. "I saw the whole thing! You just broke the **World Record for Evil Villain Speed Mummification!**"

"I'mll glllt frrr bss!" mumbled Mayor McFoodle, his mouth full of red tape.

"What'd he say?" said Einstein.

Before anyone could work it out, there was the ominous sound of timber giving way, and McFoodle tumbled through the roof directly into Lord Copperbottom's secret laboratory with a deafening crash.

There was a groaning as the whole of Grimly Towers shook.

"It's gonna blow!" shouted Kurtis. The Stunt Monkeys, Assistant Pink,

# STUNT MONKEYS

Jeremy Smashing and Miss Axelsen jumped into the golf cart and roared off the roof. As they escaped to safety, there was a loud explosion from the secret laboratory and Grimly Towers collapsed.

"Smashing!" said Jeremy, his camera trained on Grimly Towers. "Absolutely smashing!"

# CHAPTER
# FOURTEEN

## THE SANITY CLAUSE

Sludgeville had taken quite a
pounding from Mayor McFoodle and
his robotic suit. Smashed buildings;
burnt-out cars; scorched lawns. It
was even worse than the day the
Stunt Monkeys had caused The
Great SludgeFest Disaster.

The Stunt Monkeys sat on the steps

of the Town Hall and watched teams
of workmen dragging rubble into
huge trucks and carting it away. All
of Sludgeville council were working:
the Grass Inspectors, the Golf Course
Guards, the Miserable School
Caretakers Brigade. Even the Ninja
Traffic Wardens were on double duty.

"You know," said Grunt, "I'm kind
of glad we're not on TV any more."

"I know what you mean," said
Kurtis. "I can take these dumb
sunglasses off for a start."
He threw his
designer
shades into
a nearby
bin.

"And we haven't got all those cameramen poking their big noses in our business," said Einstein.

"What do we do about all these?" said Grunt. He pointed to a bunch of diehard *Stunt Mania!* fans who were hovering around. He swatted a few of them away.

"Shoo! Go on, shoo! Get out of it!"

The fans just smiled and held out their autograph books. Three or four photographers jostled for position to get a shot of the Stunt Monkeys. Even though Channel Sludge had cancelled their contract after the last stunt almost destroyed Sludgeville, the Stunt Monkeys were still big news. To say nothing of the fact that

they had saved Sludgeville from its mad mayor. A few people had even been talking about starting up a Stunt Monkeys Day. They couldn't go anywhere without being bugged by reporters, loopy fans, pushy photographers and nosy bystanders.

"You know there ought to be a rule about all this," said Grunt.

Stench and Einstein nodded.

Kurtis smiled.

"Yeah," he said. "Where's Mayor McFoodle when you need him?"

The Stunt Monkeys were still laughing when Jeremy Smashing screeched up in a large black limousine. He hopped out, followed by a small man carrying a briefcase.

"Boys!" cried Jeremy, "There's someone who'd like your autograph!"

He pushed aside a couple of photographers, and pointed at the small man. "This is my new boss, Mr Engulf N. Devour!"

The small man looked a bit like a gorilla. He stared at the Stunt Monkeys as if they were a particularly tasty bunch of bananas.

"These are the guys?" he said in an American accent, jabbing a stubby finger at the boys. "Tha ones you was telling me about?"

Jeremy Smashing nodded. "The very same! What do you think?"

Mr Devour looked at the Stunt Monkeys slowly. "You sure these are tha guys? They don't look too much from where I'm standin'."

He paused.

"But I guess if they can do half of what you say they can do, then we're in business."

He pulled a sheet of paper and pen from his briefcase.

"Sign here, here and here," he said, holding out the sheet. Grunt took the pen and signed, followed by Stench, Einstein and Kurtis.

"Congratulations, boys!" said Mr Devour. He turned and got back into his limousine.

"What did he mean, 'congratulations'?" said Kurtis. "Didn't he just want our autographs?"

Jeremy handed Kurtis a business card. It read 'Jeremy Smashing. Executive Vice President, Gigantico Pictures, Hollywood, California'.

"Of course he wanted your autographs!" said Jeremy. "On a movie contract! You're going to be stars! We're going to make millions! The company jet will be at Sludgeville Airport in an hour. Ciao!"

He turned, scampered into the limo and whizzed off at high speed.

The Stunt Monkeys watched it disappear from sight.

"Did he say 'millions'?" asked Einstein. "As in millions of dollars?"

"Parp," farted Stench, and nodded.

"What just happened?" said Grunt.

Kurtis fished his sunglasses out of the rubbish bin, and leaned back against the Town Hall steps.

"I'm not completely sure," he said, grinning. "But I'm beginning to rethink this whole fame thing! Next stop, Hollywood!"

Assistant Pink smiled and picked up a macaroon from the plate.

"Have a macaroon, Your Worship," he said, pushing it through the bars. It was visiting time at Sludgeville Jail and Assistant Pink was making his twice-weekly visit. Mayor McFoodle had been dug from the wreckage of Grimly Towers, his super-powered robot-suit broken, and all traces of his 'retraining' gone. Nothing had been found of Lord Copperbottom in the Toxic Waste Dump, although Simon Fudge-Smythe had somehow miraculously managed to escape.

"It seems you must've fallen into Copperbottom's retraining machine and reversed the transformation," said Pink. "And the lawyers tell me you should get off with a small sentence, seeing as you weren't quite yourself. Temporary insanity."

Mayor McFoodle didn't reply. He wandered over to the cell window and looked out across the exercise field. Assistant Pink tried again.

"Sir? Are you listening, sir?"

McFoodle pointed outside. "Good grief, Pink! Have you seen the length of the grass out there? We must do something about this right away!"

Assistant Pink smiled and took out his notebook. Everything was going to be just fine.